I0831412

A Father's Letter

My Sons,

I wrote this so you would know what I learned too late. The world will teach you how to win, but not how to stand tall day in and day out. It will hand you a screen instead of a mirror, applause instead of affection, freedom instead of purpose. But real love, the kind that steadies you, demands weight. It asks for presence, humility, patience, and a courage that rarely feels glamorous.

You will meet people who test every part of you. Some will ignite your fire; others will reveal your shadow. Don't run from eitherone. The flame shows what you desire. The shadow shows what you deny. Together they make you whole.

When you are tempted to chase the next bright thing, remember this: depth is the only luxury that grows with time. The rest fades like light on water.

And to my daughter, when you are old enough to read this know that your father tried to live these words so you would always recognize steadiness when you see it. Never settle for a man who wants to be admired more than he wants to be present.

With love,
Dad

Act I - The Spark

The Boy Who Burned Too Bright

At night, the city turned to glass.

Windows, billboards, bedside tables all glowing, all humming, all asking to be touched.

The Boy learned to live with a small sun in his palm. It answered when he was lonely. It applauded when he was loud. It forgave him for being afraid.

He got good at being seen.
Angles. Lighting. The right hour to post.
He could make his life look full in twelve seconds.

Sometimes he wondered if a man could starve with a banquet before him.
The answer was yes, if the food was only pictures of food.

He mistook applause for affection and pixels for proof.

He chased improvement the way other men chased sleep.
Gym at dawn. Edges sharpened. New shirt that said nothing except look at me.
He traded attention like a currency: likes for validation, stories for status, replies for the right to exist.

The phone made his wants feel clean. Simple. Swipe to try again. Swipe to forget. Swipe to become someone else.

He had spoken to a hundred women through glass and felt none of them breathe.
He was fluent in emoji, but illiterate in presence.

When the screen went dark, a reflection waited on the black pane...his own face, candlelit and hungry. The light returned and the hunger vanished. He told himself that meant he was fine.

He loved the idea of being loved.

He wasn’t looking for her.
She wasn’t looking up.

A café. Rain ticked on the window. A paperback in her hands with a cracked spine and a smudge of coffee on the corner. She didn’t perform. She didn’t check her phone. She turned pages like someone who believed in slow miracles.

He rehearsed an easy line in his head and walked by. She kept reading.
He looped the block like a coward with courage in his pockets and returned.

“Is it good?” he asked, nodding at the book.

She glanced at him, just long enough to see through the confidence he was trying on.
“It’s honest,” she said. “That makes it good.”

He felt unarmored, bare.
“Are you always that direct?”

“Only when it matters,” she said, and looked back at the page.

Her silence was louder than every cheer he’d ever earned.

He texted smoothly. In person, his tongue grew clumsy.
He knew which words could spark a thread at midnight. He didn't know what to do with a heartbeat at noon.
They met again - no filters, no soundtrack. She asked simple questions and waited for real answers.

"What do you fear?" she said.
He wanted to say poverty, failure, growing invisible.

He said, "Nothing, really," and watched the honesty slip between them like a crack forming in glass.

"Try again," she said, not unkindly.

He swallowed. "Being ordinary," he said. "And, I don't know, being truly known."

She nodded. "Those are the same fears."

He laughed like it was a joke. It wasn't.

When she smiled in person, he felt heat.
When she smiled on a screen later, he felt safe.

"You keep sending words," she wrote once, "but I'm waiting to feel a heartbeat."
No one had ever asked what lived behind his grin.

For a week he practiced presence like a foreign language.

He left his phone in the kitchen and let quiet enter the room first.

He noticed how her questions had weight, how her sentences landed and stayed instead of evaporating into noise.

They walked. Her shoulder brushed his and the contact told him more truth than a thousand messages. He caught himself wanting less performance, more proof.

He almost said it. Almost said: "I don't know how to do this. Will you teach me how to be real when you're close?"

Instead he made a joke, and her eyes dimmed by a degree he pretended not to see.

That night he scrolled through versions of her he had saved without permission...photos, phrases, the way she held a mug.
He told himself it was love.
It was a museum.

He felt naked, though he was fully dressed.

Intimacy asked something he hadn't trained for: staying.
He knew how to chase, to impress, to leave.
He didn't know how to remain when the conversation slowed and his body wanted a new hit of novelty.

He told himself he was busy. He told himself she was complicated. He told himself lies that had always worked and watched them fail.

Her silence was too loud, so he turned up the volume of everyone else.

The feed welcomed him like an old addiction.
Bodies, jokes, small wars, clipped wisdom.
Women whose names he would forget by morning. Men selling blueprints to meaning.
The easy confidence of those who never risked being touched.

Pleasure without presence became punishment.

He typed a message he wouldn't send: I think you scare me because you require me to be a person instead of a performance.
He deleted it and posted a photo of his dinner instead. People applauded. He went to bed hollow.

It happened at 2:17 a.m., in the narrow hours when the city becomes honest.

His phone froze. The screen locked with his own reflection: not the curated face, not the practiced smirk - the tired one. Eyes rimmed with blue light. Skin filmed with the day.

The darkness behind him was thicker than the room deserved.
Something in it breathed.

He lifted the phone to check the angle, and the dark breathed again, closer.
When the screen cut to black, he saw himself perfectly ringed by the shadow that had always been there, now simply unafraid to be seen.

"You wanted them to see you," a voice said. He didn't hear it with his ears. "Now they do. All of you."

He sat up. "Who's there?"
"I am," the voice said, and the word struck him like a memory.

He moved his thumb; the light returned. The shadow retreated to the corners like a loyal animal waiting for a command he did not yet know how to give.

The light made the shadow clearer.

He dreamed of falling through a quiet place. No banners, no feeds, no music telling him what to feel. Just a path at the edge of a dry plain, the horizon held together by a single thread of fire.

She stood there - the woman from the café - older somehow, or perhaps simply truer. She touched his chest with the back of her fingers, as if testing a kettle for heat.

"This is not a game," she said softly. "If you want something real, you'll have to bleed for it."

"Bleed what?" he asked.

"Pride," said another voice, the one from the dark.
"Noise," said hers.
"Dopamine," said his own voice, and the three answers braided into something he recognized as a command.

He woke before dawn with his heart racing and his phone face down on the nightstand, like a sword he wasn't sure he deserved to carry.

He went to the sink and drank water in the dark, and the house answered with the small, honest noises of pipes and wind and his own breath coming back to him after years of outsourcing it.

In the bathroom mirror, he met himself without angles.
For a long minute, they just stared - the Boy who performed and the face that would outlast performance. The shadow behind them both stood patient, like an old teacher waiting for a student to finish pretending.

He said it aloud, to no one and to the only one who could hear:
"I'm afraid of being ordinary. I'm afraid of being known."

The room did not applaud.
The silence did.

From somewhere just beyond the edge of his fear, the voice came again...low, unhurried, intimate as his own pulse:

"If you want fire," it said, "turn toward the dark that feeds it."

He switched the bathroom light off. The shadow did not disappear.
He took one breath. Then another. Then a third, like a promise.

When the sun finally touched the window, his phone lit with messages that wanted his attention. He let them wait and wrote to her instead:

I don't know how to do this yet. But I want to try in person.

He watched the three dots appear, vanish, appear again.

Okay, she wrote. Then begin.

Act II - The Descent

The Boy and The Shadow

He left the city before it could ask him why.

New streets, same glow. New names, same hunger. Nights strung together like cheap lights, then burned out.

He learned how to be wanted on command. A look, a line, the practiced lean of a shoulder. Doors opened. Beds warmed. Mornings chilled.

He told himself this was freedom - no promises, no weight.

But freedom without a direction felt like falling without a ground.

Pleasure without presence became punishment.

On a road where even the billboards were tired, he met a man walking against the wind.
Older, unhurried, eyes like cooled ash. The man looked almost familiar, like old photographs that resemble you more than mirrors do.

"Lost?" the stranger asked.

"Exploring," the Boy said.

The stranger half-smiled. "Exploring is what men call it when they're running away."

They shared a bench behind a gas station. The stranger drank water like a ritual. "What do you want?" he asked.

"To be alive," the Boy said.

The stranger nodded at the phone in his hand. "You keep asking that small sun to prove you exist."

"Who are you?" the Boy said.

"I'm the part you hide," the stranger said, gentle as a diagnosis. "I am your Shadow."

The word felt less like a threat than a relief, finally something naming him back.

They walked until the city shrank to a pulse behind them.

The Shadow spoke of hunger, its proper size, its proper place. "Hunger is innocent," he said. "It is the lies around it that make it cruel."

"I don't want to be cruel," the Boy said.

"You already are," the Shadow answered. "Cruel to yourself. You keep offering your body to strangers and withholding your heart from yourself."

They stopped where the road became dirt. "I can give you power," the Shadow said. "Not tricks. Presence. The kind that makes rooms shift when you enter. Eyes will follow. Doors will open. But it costs what you think you're protecting."

"My freedom?"

"Your illusions," the Shadow said. "The story that you can have meaning without sacrifice."

"And if I refuse?"

"You'll keep winning nights and losing years."

The promise dripped like honey over a knife. He held out his hand. The Shadow didn't shake it. He placed the Boy's own palm against his chest.

"Make a vow," the Shadow said. "Not to me—to the man you're trying to become."

The Boy swallowed. "I vow to stop lying to myself."

"Then we can begin," the Shadow said.

It arrived like gravity...quiet, undeniable. Wherever he went, attention bent. Not cheap shock, not fireworks, just presence. He could stand still, and people made space as if a storm might begin.

Conversations bloomed. Flirting felt like music he suddenly knew the notes to. Confidence moved through him like warmth.

He tested it. In a crowded bar, he said almost nothing and still became the center of attention. Eyes found him. Invitations multiplied. His chest thrummed with the old triumph...only steadier, more potent, like fire learning to burn blue.

That night, a woman traced his jaw with a single finger and whispered, “You feel...awake.”

He wanted to be worthy of that sentence.
He wasn’t.

He left before dawn, the praise still ringing and a thin cold forming under it.

Sleep thinned. Food tasted like memory.
He could command attention; he could not command peace.

Messages stacked. Bodies tangled. Laughter spilled.
Every victory was followed by a hum in his bones that he mistook for joy and later recognized as alarm.

Dreams returned, and her face was not accusing, just absent. He tried to summon her in real life and found himself rehearsing apologies for a conversation he hadn't earned.

He looked at his hands and saw the power there, and underneath the power, a tremor.

He could own any moment except the one inside his chest.

On a rooftop with a wind that smelled like electricity, he cursed the Shadow.

"You promised power."

"I delivered," the Shadow said.

"You didn't say it would hollow me out."

"You did that," the Shadow answered, unoffended. "Power is a blade. You chose where to swing it."

"I want out."

"You want discipline," the Shadow said. "You want to steer the flood instead of drowning in it."

The Boy stepped closer, furious. "Why are you helping me?"

"I'm not," the Shadow said. "I'm you when you tell the truth. I am you without the costumes."

He swung...not a fist, exactly, but something in his voice meant violence.

The Shadow did not defend. He absorbed it, like a wall that knew all storms eventually tire.

"Are you done?" the Shadow asked softly.

The Boy's shoulders collapsed. "I don't know how to be good."

"Good is a costume," the Shadow said. "Be whole."

They traveled to a place where the city's noise bled out.

A low cave with a floor of still water, so clean it looked like glass waiting for confession.

"Sit," the Shadow said.

He sat until his legs ached. He watched his reflection do nothing.

He tried to think noble thoughts. The water did not care.

He tried to catalog his sins. The water did not flinch.

He began to cry...first from frustration, then from the strange relief of not needing to perform grief. The reflection cried with him, and for the first time, he did not look away.

Silence answered him like a teacher who had waited years for this lesson.

"What now?" he whispered.

"Now we sort the fire," the Shadow said. "What part is vanity, what part is vitality, what part is violence afraid of itself."

"How?"

"By staying," said the Shadow. "This is the training you never did."

They named his hungers without shame.

Desire - not an enemy, a force.
Pride - not a crown, a shield for a frightened child.
Ambition - not a god, a tool that must be leashed to meaning.

"You don't kill fire," the Shadow said. "You give it a hearth."

"And the women?" the Boy asked, voice smaller. "How do I stop using them to prove I exist?"

"You stop auditioning," the Shadow said. "Offer presence instead of performance. Offer choice instead of pressure. Offer slowness. If you cannot be patient, you are not ready."

"That sounds like weakness."

"It is strength," the Shadow said. "A wolf that does not eat when it is hungry is no less a wolf. It is a guardian."

The Boy let the words burn through the old scripts. He saw himself like a map—roads that led to noise, paths that led to silence. He had always chosen the louder route.

"Try this," the Shadow said. "The next time desire rises, do not scroll, do not hunt, do not bargain. Breathe. Ask it what it wants for you, not from someone."

He tried. The wave came. He stood inside it. It didn't kill him. When it passed, he felt a clean soreness, like muscles after their first honest work.

Danger, once disciplined, becomes devotion.

A storm moved in, the kind that makes power flicker and dogs hide.
He walked through it with no destination, letting rain erase the latest version of himself. The streets emptied. Thunder stitched the sky.

He imagined her, how she turned pages, how her questions weighed more than his answers. He imagined returning not with a script but with a spine.

As lightning tore a seam in the clouds, he understood: the fire he feared was the same one that could keep her warm—if he learned to tend it.

He stopped at the mouth of the mirror cave and bowed without knowing why.
"I'm ready to stop running," he said.

The Shadow stepped close, close enough to blur. "Then burn," he said. "Not to be seen. To see."

Heat rose in his will. A resolve, unfamiliar and sober, took root.
He felt the first true spark of a man lighting in a boy's chest.

He turned toward the city and began the long walk home.

Act III - The Return

The Man Who Stood in Love

The city had not changed, only his eyes.

Noise still glittered, screens still begged. But where once he saw opportunity, he now saw hunger wearing perfume.

He found her where sunlight met the smell of coffee...same table, same book, new calm.
She looked up; surprise softened into recognition.

"You came back."

"I finally left," he said.

She closed her book. The pause between them felt clean.

She no longer needed his fire; she could tell he'd become its keeper.

They walked beside the river that sliced the city like a scar.

He told her about the Shadow, the bargains, the noise he had mistaken for life.

He didn't ask for forgiveness; he asked for clarity.

"I wanted to conquer love," he said. "Now I want to serve it."
She studied him. "Then serve by staying honest. Not perfect, just present."

He nodded, the first vow made without spectacle.

"Presence," he said. "That's the only luxury I still believe in."

They shared a single honest embrace. A closure, not a conquest.

There was no music, only traffic and their breathing.

In holding her, he felt the hum of every choice that had brought him here.

He understood that love was not a rescue; it was a responsibility freely chosen, every day, without applause.

In holding her, he held the man he had become.

That night, alone, he sat in the dark.
The Shadow waited—not looming, not whispering. Simply there.

"Are we finished?" the Boy asked.

"We are begun," the Shadow said.

It stepped forward and dissolved into him, like smoke returning to its source.
Heat spread through his chest, steady, contained.

The beast now guarded the temple it once threatened.

He realized mastery was not control—it was cooperation.

He no longer fought his nature; he directed it.

Years blurred into work, laughter, quiet repetition.

He built things that lasted, like tables, trust, and a rhythm.

Each morning, he rose before the screens. He practiced silence like a craft.

Devotion became discipline; discipline became peace.
He no longer chased meaning; he maintained it.

"Love," he wrote in a worn notebook, "is not a feeling to find, but a craft to practice.

Devotion is just discipline done with an open heart."

One evening a young man knocked at his door...restless eyes, phone glowing in his hand.

"I've read about you," the pilgrim said. "People say you never fall, you always stand in the light. How do you resist temptation?"

He smiled. "I stopped resisting. I repurposed my flame."

The boy frowned. "What does that mean?"

"It means I gave my hunger the job to build, not to burn."

The pilgrim left with more questions than he'd brought. That was the point.

Later that night he wrote a letter on real paper, words meant to outlive batteries:

"For every boy who mistakes hunger for passion.

Your Flame is innocent. Do not shame it.
Teach it loyalty, and it will light your world.
Feed it lies, and it will consume you.

The Shadow is not your enemy; it is your untrained strength.

Find someone whose calm challenges your noise, and stand beside them until you learn to hear the quiet."

He folded the letter and sealed it with a thumbprint of ash.

Epilogue

The Flame

Years later, in another apartment in another glowing city, a boy found the letter inside an old notebook.

He read it while the room hummed with notifications.

He turned his phone face-down.
For a moment, silence introduced itself.

He looked out at the neon night, thinking of fire and shadows and the strange inheritance of men who finally learn to stay.

And in that pause - before the next vibration, before the next scroll -

a small spark inside him whispered: "begin"

THE END

(AND THE BEGINNING)

AUTHOR'S NOTE

This story was written in the language of parable but born from the everyday work of being human. Every man carries both shadow and flame; the task is not to banish one or the other, but to learn their dance. If you found yourself somewhere in these pages...keep going. The world needs men who can burn bright without burning others.

-Steven Patrick Sakadales

The Shadow and the Flame

For permission requests, contact:
Dragon Rider Publishing
452 E Thurman Mill St
Garden City, Idaho, 83714 USA

www.ingramcontent.com/pod-product-compliance
Lightning Source LLC
Chambersburg PA
CBHW060759310726
48980CB00002B/162

* 9 7 9 8 9 9 3 6 4 7 6 1 6 *